THE GREAT PATTY CAPER

adapted by Erica David
based on the screenplay by Casey Alexander, Zeus Cervas,
Steven Banks, and Dani Michaeli
illustrated by Stephen Reed

SIMON SPOTLIGHT/NICKELODEON
New York   London   Toronto   Sydney

Stephen Hillenburg

Based on the TV series *SpongeBob SquarePants*™ created by Stephen Hillenburg as seen on Nickelodeon™

SIMON SPOTLIGHT/NICKELODEON

An imprint of Simon & Schuster Children's Publishing Division

1230 Avenue of the Americas, New York, New York 10020

For information about special discounts for bulk purchases, please contact Simon & Schuster Special Sales

at 1-866-506-1949 or business@simonandschuster.com.

Manufactured in the United States of America 0611 LAK

10 9 8 7 6 5 4 3 2

ISBN 978-1-4424-0781-7

It was a very special day for Mr. Krabs. "SpongeBob, me boy, I have something important to tell you," he said.

"What is it, Mr. Krabs?" SpongeBob asked.

"I've finally found a way to keep Plankton from stealing me secret Krabby Patty formula," Mr. Krabs replied. "I've sent it far, far away where he'll never be able to find it!"

"That's great, Mr. Krabs!" SpongeBob said. Then he frowned. "But we just ran out of Krabby Patties and we need the formula to make more!"

"Ah, tartar sauce!" Mr. Krabs grumbled. "The formula's all the way on the opposite side of the ocean!"

"I'll get it, Mr. Krabs," SpongeBob said. "Send me! I won't let you down."

"This is a very important mission, boy. The formula is in a safe-deposit box in the ocean's largest and safest bank, in Way Far-Out Townville," Mr. Krabs explained. He pulled out a key from his pocket. "This is the key to the box. Guard it with your life, SpongeBob."

"Aye, aye, sir!" SpongeBob said, determined to do his best.

Later that day, SpongeBob and Patrick boarded the Oceanic Express to go to Way Far-Out Townville. Little did they know that Plankton was following them.

"Remember, Patrick," SpongeBob said. "This is an important mission. Keep your eyes open for any suspicious characters."

SpongeBob and Patrick walked through the train to the dining car.

"Hey, SpongeBob, does that guy look suspicious to you?" Patrick whispered. "I think he might be spying on us!"

SpongeBob chuckled. Patrick was staring at his own reflection!

"Relax, Pat. I don't think *he* will give us any trouble," SpongeBob replied.

A man walked up to them. "I'm sorry, but the dining car is closed," he said in a snooty way.

"But we haven't even heard the specials yet!" SpongeBob said.

"No! The dining car is over for *you*. You must leave now!" the man snapped.

He grabbed SpongeBob and Patrick and tossed them out of the dining car.

"Well, that was certainly suspicious!" SpongeBob exclaimed. "Patrick, we'll have to find a safe place to store this for the night."

He reached into his pocket for the key, but couldn't find it! "The key! It's gone!" he yelled.

Just then, SpongeBob spotted Plankton. "Plankton, *you* stole the key!" he said.
"I just got here! I couldn't have stolen it . . . yet," Plankton said with an evil grin.
"I don't believe you. Search him, Patrick," SpongeBob ordered.
Patrick lifted Plankton up and shook him upside down. "He's clean," Patrick said.
"Then someone *else* on this train must have stolen the key!" SpongeBob said.

SpongeBob and Patrick called the police and rounded up the suspects.

"I think I know who did it," SpongeBob said. "Mr. Police Chief, I submit to you the nanny! Search this baby's diaper and you'll find the key."

The police chief searched—and found a stolen diamond in the baby's diaper!

"Great job, Mr. SquarePants! You nabbed the infamous Jewel Triplets Gang!" the inspector said.

"Hmm, if they didn't do it, then it has to be the butler," said SpongeBob. "The butler always commits the crime! Shake him down!"

When the police chief revealed that the "butler" had been wearing a mask, the cop exclaimed, "It's Oren J. Roughy! He's an international fugitive wanted for stealing more than seventy-five thousand dollars worth of ham sandwiches! Thank you, Mr. SquarePants!"

"You're welcome, but what about the key? I've failed Mr. Krabs!" SpongeBob wailed.

"Don't worry, it'll turn up," Patrick replied as he pulled something out of his pocket and began to pick his teeth with it.

"Patrick, that's the key! Where did you find it?" SpongeBob asked.

"I found it when I was cleaning your shorts earlier," Patrick answered.

"Oh," SpongeBob said sheepishly.

With the key found, SpongeBob and Patrick settled down for a nap. "Would you mind scooching over, SpongeBob?" Patrick asked. "I can't even move my eyebrows."

"I'm trying, Patrick, but it's really cramped. This isn't exactly Bikini Bottom!" SpongeBob said.

Suddenly Plankton popped up from under the covers. "Need more room?" he asked, opening the window. "Maybe I can help."

"What a cool view," Patrick said.

"Have a better look," said Plankton. Then he pushed SpongeBob and Patrick right out of the window. "So long. And thanks for the key!"

"What are we going to do, SpongeBob?" Patrick asked.

"Follow that train!" SpongeBob said.

They ran after the train until they came to the edge of a cliff. The train pulled away from them and followed the tracks into a canyon below.

"Uh-oh. Now what?" Patrick asked.

"Not to worry, Patrick. I have an idea," SpongeBob said. He grabbed Patrick and jumped off the side of the cliff.

"Ahhhhhhh!" Patrick screamed.

But SpongeBob just smiled as he flopped and flapped—and changed into the shape of a hang glider!

They soon landed safely on the roof of the train.

SpongeBob and Patrick climbed down into the train. They chased Plankton from one car to the next.

"You won't get away with this Plankton!" said SpongeBob.

Finally SpongeBob and Patrick chased Plankton all the way to the front of the train.

"All right, Plankton, end of the line!" SpongeBob cried.

"For you, maybe," Plankton replied as he quickly unhitched the engine from the passenger cars.

"Uh-oh, Patrick, we've got a big problem!" SpongeBob said. "We're on a runaway train!"

"Quick, look around. There has to be a way to stop this thing!"
SpongeBob told Patrick.

Patrick stared at the control panel. He found a lever labeled BRAKE.

"Don't worry, SpongeBob, I'll save us!" he said. Patrick grabbed the
lever and jerked it back and forth until it broke! He proudly showed
SpongeBob the broken handle.

THE GREAT PATTY CAPER

Meanwhile Plankton sneaked into the Way Far-Out Townville Bank.
He used the key to open the safe-deposit box. "At last, my day of triumph
has come!" he said.

As he picked up the Krabby Patty formula, a voice called out, "Just a
minute, Plankton."

Mr. Krabs stepped out from the shadows. "Did you honestly think I
wouldn't have planned for you?"

Plankton sighed as he handed over the formula. "Just keeping it warm
for you, Krabs."

"Patrick, you broke the brake!" SpongeBob cried.

"It told me to," Patrick replied.

The train kept speeding down the tracks, and SpongeBob and Patrick were helpless to stop it! It burst through a train station and looped through the dreaded Twisted Trestles.